MESSY
Miranda

MESSY Miranda

Jeff Szpirglas AND Danielle Saint-Onge

ILLUSTRATED BY Dave Whamond

ORCA BOOK PUBLISHERS

Library and Archives Canada Cataloguing in Publication

Szpirglas, Jeff, author
Messy Miranda / Jeff Szpirglas, Danielle Saint-Onge ;
illustrated by Dave Whamond.
(Orca echoes)

Issued in print and electronic formats.
ISBN 978-1-4598-0117-2 (pbk.).--ISBN 978-1-4598-0118-9 (pdf).
ISBN 978-1-4598-0518-7 (epub)

I. Saint-Onge, Danielle, author II. Whamond, Dave, illustrator
III. Title. IV. Series: Orca echoes
PS8637.Z65M48 2013   jC813'.6   C2013-902336-4
C2013-902337-2

First published in the United States, 2013
Library of Congress Control Number: 2013937059

Summary: Miranda can't seem to get a handle on the mess in her desk,
until she finds a magical solution to her problem.

Orca Book Publishers gratefully acknowledges the support for its publishing programs
provided by the following agencies: the Government of Canada through the Canada Book Fund
and the Canada Council for the Arts, and the Province of British Columbia
through the BC Arts Council and the Book Publishing Tax Credit.

MIX
Paper from
responsible sources
FSC® C004071

*Orca Book Publishers is dedicated to preserving the environment and
has printed this book on Forest Stewardship Council® certified paper.*

Cover artwork and interior illustrations by Dave Whamond
Author photo by Tim Basile

ORCA BOOK PUBLISHERS   ORCA BOOK PUBLISHERS
PO Box 5626, STN. B   PO Box 468
Victoria, BC Canada   Custer, WA USA
V8R 6S4   98240-0468

www.orcabook.com
Printed and bound in Canada.

16 15 14 13 • 4 3 2 1

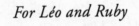

For Léo and Ruby

Chapter One

"All right, class," said Ms. Basil, "it's time to clean out your desks."

Miranda got nervous whenever Ms. Basil said that. It was the weekly desk cleanup. She hated desk cleanup more than spelling tests. She hated it more than fixing her writing. In fact, Miranda could not think of anything she hated more.

Other students loved the weekly desk cleanup, which happened every Friday. Neela used that time to sharpen her pencils, since her desk was always neat and tidy. She never shoved loose papers inside, or broken pencils, or leftover lunch. No dirt ever came near her desk.

Miranda's desk was another story.

Ms. Basil came by Miranda's desk and bent down. She took a long look inside. "Miranda, what's in your desk?"

"My books," Miranda said.

"And...?"

"My pencils."

"And...?"

"My science project."

"And...?"

"Some other stuff." Miranda's face started turning red.

"A *lot* of stuff, I'd say," Ms. Basil said. She stood up straight and crossed her arms. "Too much stuff."

Miranda gulped. She looked over to Neela and her friends. They were already at the door, waiting for the recess bell. Neela had a bright-orange skipping rope in her hand.

"Hey, Miranda, are you going to skip with us at recess?"

Miranda nodded her head. "Just a minute."

CRASH!

Miranda jumped. She and Ms. Basil turned to see Jaiden's desk tipped over on its side. The contents had spilled out and spread across the floor. Now the floor was a mess of crumpled paper and pencil bits.

Jaiden always found cool things during the weekly desk cleanup. Interesting bits of junk somehow made their way inside his desk. Now he was looking at a dried-up apple core. How did it get there? It was a mystery, and Jaiden was hungry. He took a bite. Jaiden wasn't afraid to eat anything.

Miranda let out a high-pitched "Ewwwww!"

Jaiden gulped down the apple bit. He looked at Miranda. "I was hungry. What's in your desk, Miranda? Anything good?"

Miranda shook her head.

"You won't know until you dump it," Jaiden said.

Some kids near Jaiden started to chant, "Dump it! Dump it!"

Ms. Basil cleared her throat. "Jaiden, you will be staying in the classroom until you clean up your mess."

Jaiden's smile fell. "But recess is in five minutes."

"Yes," Ms. Basil said firmly.

"It will take at least fifteen minutes to clean this mess up."

"Yes." Ms. Basil did not need to raise her voice to make a point.

"Oh," Jaiden said. "I guess I'm staying in."

"Don't worry," Ms. Basil said. "Miranda will keep you company."

Miranda eyed Neela's skipping rope. "But I want to go skipping."

Ms. Basil bent down to look into Miranda's desk again. A piece of Miranda's science project fell to the floor. "You can go skipping as soon as your desk is tidy." She smiled.

The recess bell rang.

"See you later, Miranda!" said Neela.

Miranda lowered her head and stared at her desk. How was she ever going to tidy up?

Chapter Two

Miranda missed recess. As she cleaned, she looked out the window. She watched Neela and her friends skip rope. Everybody looked so happy playing outside. Jaiden was even happy exploring his mess. He took crumpled papers and shot them into the garbage bin like a basketball player. Ms. Basil just sat by the window, reading a book and enjoying the sunshine.

It took all of recess for Miranda to clean up her desk.

Miranda was so upset that she didn't smile the rest of the school day. Her backpack was stuffed with the mess she'd cleaned out. It was so heavy, Miranda zigzagged all the way down the hall to her brother's class. Ben was in grade six and always walked home with her.

Ben scooped up her backpack and slung it over his shoulder. "Let me guess. Desk cleanup."

Miranda nodded slowly. She was close to tears.

"You missed recess again."

Miranda nodded. "I didn't get to skip rope with Neela."

Ben put his arm around Miranda. "Here's the good news. It's Friday night, and we're going to see Uncle Aldo."

That took the frown off Miranda's face.

Friday-night dinner with Uncle Aldo was the best!

Uncle Aldo was the coolest uncle in the world. He was a real magician. He knew all sorts of card tricks. He could make a coin appear from behind your ear. He could even pull a rabbit out of a hat!

One thing Uncle Aldo couldn't do was cook. He was too busy making magic to worry about food.

That was fine. It meant Friday night was also pizza night!

Miranda, Ben and their parents showed up with two boxes of steaming-hot pizza. Uncle Aldo opened the door wearing a bright sparkly suit. He had a wild moustache and a few streaks of white in his hair. "Presto!" he said.

"Presto, Uncle Aldo!" Ben said. Uncle Aldo never said *hello*.

"Do I smell pizza?" asked Uncle Aldo.

"What gives you that idea?" said Miranda's dad, holding the pizza boxes.

"Magic," said Uncle Aldo, smiling.

Miranda and her family stepped inside. Uncle Aldo lived in a small house in the city. The living room was cluttered with rabbit and bird cages. Uncle Aldo kept the animals for his act here. There were shelves full of magic books, wands and colored scarves tied together. It was the best house ever.

Uncle Aldo bent down to give Miranda a hug. "How was your day?"

Miranda shook her head. "I missed recess."

"Again?"

Miranda nodded.

Uncle Aldo smiled. "I know what to do." He reached behind her ear and pulled out a big shiny coin. "Presto! Magic will solve the problem!"

Miranda's mom shook her head. "Aldo, won't pizza solve the problem instead?"

Uncle Aldo's stomach growled. "Good idea. Let's eat."

He led the family into the kitchen. They all sat at the table and had dinner.

As she ate her pizza, Miranda kept thinking about the mess in her desk. She wondered about what Uncle Aldo had said.

Could magic solve the problem?

There was one way to find out.

Chapter Three

After dinner, Uncle Aldo wanted to show Miranda and her family his new trick.

Ben's eyes lit up. "When can you teach me? I want to show everybody at school," he said. "I'd be the best at it."

Uncle Aldo smiled. "What do I always tell you? Magic isn't a game," he said. "You need to be careful. There's a lot of power in magic tricks."

Uncle Aldo reached into his pocket. "Presto!" he shouted. He pulled out a huge bunch of flowers. He gave them to Miranda's mom. "What do you think?"

The flowers squirted water at Miranda's mom.

"Ooops!" said Uncle Aldo.

"Ooops is right," said Miranda's mom. "You still need to practice."

Miranda pushed her chair away from the table. "I'll be right back," she said. "I have to go to the bathroom."

While Uncle Aldo practiced his new trick, Miranda left the kitchen and walked up the stairs. The bathroom was on the second floor. But so was Uncle Aldo's magic room. Miranda didn't really need to go to the bathroom. What she needed was magic.

Miranda knew she shouldn't go into Uncle Aldo's magic room alone. It was his special place, where he kept his secrets. But Miranda needed to fix her messy-desk problem for good. Magic would do the trick!

The stairs were creaky. She walked as quietly as she could. The floor just outside the magic room creaked so loudly that Miranda stopped. Her heart skipped a beat. She listened. Uncle Aldo was still doing his tricks downstairs. Nobody had heard her.

Then she opened the door.

SQUEEEEAK.

Miranda's hand shook as she opened the door. She had never been in here by herself.

The magic room seemed bigger than the whole top floor. How could it be so big? Magic, Miranda thought.

In the room were dusty shelves full of old wands, lengths of chain and battered trunks. Sitting on a small table was a row of top hats. Miranda knew that Uncle Aldo could pull rabbits out of those hats. She had seen him do this many times.

If a rabbit could go into the hat, what else could? Maybe the mess from her desk? But how would she sneak the hat out? She couldn't wear it down the stairs. Could she flatten the hat and put it into her pocket?

Miranda pushed down on the middle hat as hard as she could.

A small white rabbit leaped out of the hat.

Miranda jumped back.

The rabbit just looked at her and twitched its whiskers. Then it jumped into another hat on the same table.

Uncle Aldo had so many top hats. He didn't need all of them, did he?

Miranda looked down. She had squashed the hat into a flat disk. She put her hand in. Wow! It looked like her hand was going right into the table. It disappeared up to her wrist. She pulled her hand back out and wiggled her fingers. "Presto!" Miranda smiled. It was time to make some magic of her own.

Chapter Four

Miranda woke up Monday morning feeling great. She was going to solve her messy-desk problem once and for all!

She was in such a good mood at breakfast that she ate two big bowls of cereal. She even skipped to school beside Ben. "Why are you so happy?" he said. "It's Monday and I have a math test. I forgot to study."

"Today I'm going to skip with Neela at *every* recess." Miranda smiled.

When Miranda and Ben got to school, Ben shuffled over to his friends. They were listening to music and bopping their heads. They all looked tired.

Miranda saw Neela coming off the school bus. Neela already had her skipping rope ready in her hand. Miranda ran to greet her.

"Are you going to skip with us today?" Neela asked.

Miranda gave her a big smile. "I will now *and* at recess too."

A few more girls showed up. Talia and Penny each took hold of one end of the rope. They started to twirl it. Neela jumped first. She was amazing!

Miranda had spent so many recesses inside that she needed some skipping practice. She needed to practice her skipping like Uncle Aldo needed to practice his magic.

"Come on in!" Neela said.

Miranda jumped in. As the rope twirled, she skipped. She watched Neela bounce up and down with her. "You're great!" Neela said.

Miranda's smile felt as wide as the skipping rope was long.

Finally, she and Neela jumped to the side so the other girls could skip. As she did, Miranda felt something fall from her pocket. It was the magic hat!

It rolled across the pavement and knocked into Jaiden's feet.

"Oh no!" Miranda said.

Jaiden bent down to pick it up. He sniffed it. He looked around and gave it a private lick. Then he noticed Miranda was staring at him.

"Jaiden, give that back. It's mine!"

The hat was still flattened like a pancake. Jaiden pretended to throw it. "Nice Frisbee, Miranda!"

Miranda stormed up to him. "It's not a toy!" she said. She didn't want Jaiden to find out that the hat was really magical.

But Jaiden threw the hat over to his friend Abdu. Abdu caught it and tossed it over to another boy. Soon the boys were playing Frisbee with it.

How was Miranda going to stop them? If they found out the hat was magic, they would take it away. Or worse.

Miranda saw Ms. Basil out in the yard. If she told Ms. Basil, maybe the boys would give the hat back.

Just as Miranda was going over to her, Jaiden caught the hat. He saw Ms. Basil watching them. Her arms were folded across her chest. She was shaking her head back and forth. "Wait, Miranda!" Jaiden said.

Miranda stopped and saw Jaiden holding the hat. "Here. I was just kidding," he said.

Miranda snatched the hat from Jaiden. She shoved it back into her pocket.

"It's just a hat," Miranda said. But she jammed her hand into her pocket to keep it safe.

The bell rang. Miranda quickly took her backpack and lined up at the door. She stole a glance over her shoulder. Jaiden was giving her a funny look. It seemed like he was watching her every move.

Would he see her put the hat into her desk?

Miranda was going to have to be sneaky about this.

Chapter Five

As the students entered the classroom, Miranda dashed to her seat. She sat down and started pulling books out of her desk.

Neela saw this. "Why are you taking out your textbooks? It's not desk cleanup day today."

"I'm trying to stay organized, Neela," Miranda said. "I can't keep missing recess."

But that wasn't the real reason. Miranda needed to put the hat at the bottom of her desk. She looked over her shoulder. Ms. Basil was busy helping Abdu take off his boots. They were stuck on tight and on the wrong feet.

It was time!

With nobody watching, Miranda slowly pulled the crumpled hat from her pocket. She smoothed it back into a flat disk and slid it into the desk with its brim facing up. She pushed the hat to the back of her desk so it would not be seen. Then she took her books and placed them on top of the hat.

The books fell right into the hole in her desk. Perfect! She could fit all sorts of things into the magic hat. Just how much could she fit? Miranda was going to find out. Today was book exchange at the library. Miranda was going to try a little experiment.

Just then a shadow fell across Miranda's desk. She turned around. Jaiden was standing there. He was chewing on the end of a pencil. The pointy end! He pulled it out of his mouth and licked his lips. "That desk is really clean, Miranda," he said. He had a funny smile on his face, like he knew Miranda was up to something. "Can I see?"

"Uh, sure," Miranda said.

Jaiden bent down low to get a good look. He sniffed the inside of the desk. "Smells different today," he said.

"Uh, I guess," Miranda said. Her heart beat faster.

"Where's that Frisbee thing you brought?"

"My bag!" Miranda said quickly. "And don't even think about touching it!"

Jaiden stood up suddenly. He backed away. Miranda followed Jaiden's gaze. He was staring at Ms. Basil, who had come by. Ms. Basil looked down at Miranda's desk. Now it was her turn to inspect it. "Wow, Miranda! It sure looks clean in there. I hope it stays that way until Friday."

"Oh, it *will*," Miranda said.

As Ms. Basil walked away, Miranda tore a page out of her reading journal. She crumpled it into a ball. Then she threw it into the desk and pushed it over to the hat. The paper vanished into the hole. The mess was gone. This was going to be a fun week!

As the day went on, Miranda practiced making things appear and disappear. During math, she put her ruler into the hat. When nobody was looking, she pulled it back out again. "Presto!" Miranda said.

Everybody in the class looked at Miranda.

"Presto?" Ms. Basil said. "I thought we were doing a measuring lesson. Not magic."

"Sorry, Ms. Basil. My ruler is just so much fun today." Miranda smiled.

"I hope it is fun every day," Ms. Basil said.

After that, the students broke into small groups to measure different objects in the classroom. Jaiden measured a half-eaten cheese sandwich from the previous week. Neela was measuring her skipping rope with a big yardstick. "Wow!" Neela said. "It's three times longer than the yardstick. Come see, Miranda."

Miranda went over to see what Neela was doing. Her eyes widened when she saw the yardstick. "Hey, Neela. May I borrow that for a minute?"

"Sure," Neela said. "Can I come?"

Miranda shook her head. "I'll be right back." She didn't want Neela to find out about the hat.

Miranda took the yardstick and went back to her desk. When nobody was looking, she slowly dipped the stick into her desk and into the hat. Wow! The hat was at least three feet deep.

"What are you doing?" Jaiden asked.

Miranda jumped. As she did so, the yardstick came flying out of her desk. It clattered to the floor in front of Jaiden's feet.

Jaiden dropped his sandwich. "Yowzers! That's crazy!"

"These desks sure are big," Miranda said. She smiled at Jaiden.

Jaiden scratched his head. "Uh, I guess."

Ms. Basil clapped her hands. Everyone clapped back and looked at her.

"It's time for book exchange at the library."

Everyone cheered. The library was the best!

Miranda smiled. It was time to see what else she could fit into the hat.

Chapter Six

The library was full of books. Big books, little books, heavy books, thin books. There were sports books, monster books, princess books, volcano books. There were books about everything — bugs, cooking and even skipping. Miranda had read many of them. Today she wanted *The Biggest Book of Big Things*. It was the biggest book in the whole library, and she had a plan.

It was tricky to sign it out, because there was never any place you could put it. The book was taller than the kids in grade three. It had to go on a special shelf in the library. When Miranda took it down, she nearly fell over. She had to tuck it under her arm and drag it to the librarian.

"Are you sure you want that book?" the librarian asked.

"Oh, I'm sure!" Miranda said.

"You could use that book for a surfboard," Jaiden said. He pretended to surf on one of the chairs.

"Jaiden, get down!" Ms. Basil said.

As Ms. Basil took care of Jaiden, the librarian signed out *The Biggest Book of Big Things*. Inside were all sorts of pictures of big things, like dinosaurs, skyscrapers, airplanes and whales. Miranda did not care much about them. She had only signed out *The Biggest Book of Big Things* to see if it would fit into the hat in her desk.

The students lined up and marched back to class.

Miranda had to get Neela to help her carry the book back. "How are you going to get this home?" Neela asked.

Miranda shrugged. "Ben can help me." But Miranda had no plans to take the book home.

As soon as everyone had entered the classroom, the recess bell rang. "Quickly, students," Ms. Basil said. "I have recess duty!" She did not have time to help the students put things away. Instead, Ms. Basil threw on her coat. She put on her orange safety vest and dashed out of the room.

This was perfect! Miranda stayed behind until everybody had left. Then she tried to put *The Biggest Book of Big Things* into her desk.

She started by putting in a corner of the book. Then she put in the first half. Soon the whole book had slipped into the magic hat without making a sound.

Miranda's jaw dropped. "Wow!" she said. "Magic is so cool!"

Now that the book was safe in the hat, Miranda turned to go outside. She stopped in her tracks. Jaiden was standing just outside the door. His eyes were wide as Frisbees. "No way!" he said.

Miranda shook her head. "I told you these desks are big."

Jaiden scratched his head. "But that's *The Biggest Book of Big Things*," he said. "There's no way it can fit into a desk."

"It just did," Miranda said. She tried not to look nervous as she walked out of the classroom past Jaiden. She did not want him to go near her desk or find out her secret. She was going to have to be very careful. But first, she was going to skip with Neela.

Back at home after school, Miranda got a phone call from Uncle Aldo.

"Miranda, have you seen my magic hat? I can't find it anywhere."

Miranda felt her heart beat quickly. She swallowed hard. "Don't you have a bunch of magic hats?"

"Yes, but I've lost my most magical hat," he said. "One of my rabbits is still in there." Uncle Aldo explained that he had found one of the two rabbits that fit into the hat. But the hat and the other rabbit were missing.

"Oh no," Miranda said. She didn't know what to do. If she told Uncle Aldo about the hat, he would be angry with her. Plus, Miranda's desk would get messy again. Ms. Basil would keep her in for recess.

Miranda needed to think about this.

"I'll look around for it," she said. "Maybe Ben borrowed it to practice magic."

Uncle Aldo paused. "Really? But he was downstairs with us the whole night."

"Oh," Miranda said. "You're right." She couldn't think of anything else to say. "I will look for it, Uncle Aldo." She hung up the phone.

Miranda felt bad about lying to her uncle. She didn't like telling lies, and she had been telling them all day long.

As good as the day had been, now she was worried about the hat. Was there a real rabbit inside? If so, she would have to feed it tomorrow!

Miranda snuck into the kitchen to find a few special treats.

Chapter Seven

In class the next day, all Miranda could think about was the poor bunny rabbit. It would be hungry. And had she squashed it with *The Biggest Book of Big Things*? She hoped not.

First, she had to try feeding it.

While Ms. Basil was teaching a lesson about healthy food choices, Miranda reached into her pocket and pulled out a carrot stick. She kept her eyes on the teacher and slowly slipped her hand into the desk. She felt around for the hat. There it was! Her arm vanished into the hat. It was like somebody had put a giant hole in the bottom of the desk. She stretched her whole arm in. She waited for the bunny.

"Miranda?" a voice called. It was Ms. Basil.

Miranda pulled her hand out quickly.

"Can you think of a healthy food choice?" she asked.

Had Ms. Basil seen her? Miranda started to sweat. "Uh, carrots?"

"Good answer." Ms. Basil nodded. "Who else can think of a healthy food choice?"

"Pizza with ice cream and gummy spiders!" Jaiden said.

The class started to laugh.

Miranda reached into her pocket for another carrot. She put her hand back into the desk and dropped the carrot into the hat. She took another. And another.

"Miranda?" a voice called again. "What are you putting into your desk?" It was Ms. Basil.

"Nothing!" Miranda said. She took out her hands and held them up.

Ms. Basil stared at her for a moment. Then she got the class to start an activity.

Miranda didn't know how she was going to sneak the hat out. She had to get it back to Uncle Aldo soon. Maybe she could grab it quickly when no one was looking. She was going to have to wait until recess.

"I know what you're doing," a voice said. It was not Ms. Basil. It was Jaiden. He stood behind Miranda and peeked into her desk. "You're putting food inside. I saw you."

Miranda shook her head.

"Yes you did."

"Okay," Miranda said. "I did. I was saving carrots for later."

"Can I have some?" Jaiden asked.

"No, they're for later."

"I'm so hungry," Jaiden said. "I can't wait for snack time." He pushed Miranda aside and peered into the desk again. This time, his whole head fit inside it. "Wow, it really is a big desk. How did that happen? And it's so neat too!"

"Jaiden, get *out* of my desk!" Miranda yelled. "You're going to get in trouble."

Jaiden wasn't listening. "I can fit my whole neck in too! This is cool. But where are the carrots?"

Jaiden pushed himself farther into the desk. Now just his legs were sticking out. People around were starting to notice. Some pointed. "That's crazy!" said Abdu. "Ms. Basil, look at what Jaiden is doing!"

Miranda turned. Ms. Basil had wide eyes. Her mouth had dropped open. "I don't believe it!" Ms. Basil said. She stormed over to Miranda's desk.

By now, Jaiden's feet were wiggling at the mouth of the desk. Miranda tried to pull Jaiden back, but he was too far in. And too heavy.

"I found the carrots! But something is eating them. Something fluffy and white!"

The whole class had gathered around Miranda's desk. Nobody could believe what they were seeing. Nobody except Miranda.

"Hey!" Jaiden said. "Give those carrots back. I'm hungry!!!"

Jaiden's feet slipped out of Miranda's hands as he pushed himself deeper into the magic hat.

"I'm falllllllling!" Jaiden said. His voice trailed away.

Miranda reached out to grab him, but it was too late. Jaiden had vanished into her desk!

Chapter Eight

"Jaiden, get out of that desk right now!" Ms. Basil said. "Or else...or else I'm going to call the principal!" Ms. Basil tried to sound angry, but Miranda could tell she didn't know what to do. Ms. Basil tried again. "I'm going to count to ten. One...two..."

Miranda knew the magic hat was deep. If she tried to lean in and grab Jaiden, she might fall in too. Miranda peered into her desk. "Jaiden, are you okay?"

"Yeah!" he said. His voice echoed up from deep inside her desk. "It's really big down here. But there's a lot of junk. And *The Biggest Book of Big Things*. And a bunny too!"

"Jaiden, I'm coming to get you," Miranda said, using her bravest voice. She was afraid of falling into the hat, but this was her mess. She needed to clean it up.

She moved away from the desk and looked around the room. She saw Neela standing there and had an idea. "Neela! Go get your skipping rope. The one that's bigger than three yardsticks."

Neela nodded. She ran to her bag and brought it over.

"Good," Miranda said. She gave one end to Neela. "Tie one end to the desk."

"What are you going to do?" Neela asked.

"I'm going to rescue Jaiden!"

Ms. Basil was busy trying to get all the students to return to their seats. She did not see Neela tie one end of her skipping rope to a desk nearby. She also did not see Miranda squeeze into the desk, holding on to the other end of the rope.

Miranda lowered herself into the hole in her desk. It was so dark inside that she couldn't tell where the desk ended and the magic hat began. Everything was pitch-black except for the skipping rope. Cool! It glowed in the dark!

That meant she could use it like a night-light to find Jaiden.

"Jaiden, are you down there?"

For a moment, Miranda didn't hear anything.

Then came Jaiden's voice. "Is that a glow-in-the-dark skipping rope? Coooool!"

"Jaiden!" Miranda snapped. "Grab on. I'm going to get you out of here."

"Who says I want to get out?"

Miranda huffed. She had to think of something. The magic hat was not safe. Then her eyes lit up. "Jaiden, Ms. Basil just handed out some snacks."

At once Miranda felt a tug on the skipping rope. "Hurry up, Miranda. Snack time is my favorite part of the day!"

Climbing down the skipping rope was easy, but it was hard to get back up. Miranda had to squeeze her head through the narrow desk. She had to pull her body through, and it didn't want to fit. Then she felt a pair of hands grab her arms and yank her out. Miranda spilled onto the floor. She looked up to see Neela standing there. "You did it!" Neela said.

A second later, there was a loud thump. Jaiden crashed onto the floor beside her. He was holding *The Biggest Book of Big Things*. Sitting on his head was a white rabbit. It bounced off and hopped across the floor.

The class cheered. "Dump the desk! Dump the desk!"

Ms. Basil shook her head. "There will be no more desk-dumping."

Miranda let out a big sigh. She had done it. Jaiden and the bunny were safe.

Chapter Nine

That night Miranda's parents drove her to see Uncle Aldo. Miranda brought the rabbit and the hat up to the front door. She was scared to tell Uncle Aldo the truth. What would he say? Miranda took a deep breath and knocked.

Uncle Aldo did not look pleased when he opened the door and saw Miranda holding the rabbit and the hat.

"I'm sorry I took the hat without asking," Miranda said. She held her head down low. She felt him take the hat and the rabbit from her hands. Her eyes filled with tears.

Then she felt a warm hand on her shoulder. She looked up. Uncle Aldo was smiling. "I'm glad

you brought it back," he said as he straightened the hat out. It had been squashed in the desk and looked a bit funny. "It was the right thing to do. But what happened to the hat?"

Miranda told Uncle Aldo about her messy desk, and how she'd thought that magic would solve the problem.

"I know what you mean," Uncle Aldo said. Miranda followed him into the house. "See?" he said. "My place is a huge mess. I always have trouble keeping it clean."

"Do you use magic too?"

Uncle Aldo shook his head. "You have to be careful with magic."

Miranda looked around the living room. There were pizza boxes on the floor. Papers were scattered everywhere. "This looks just like my desk," Miranda said, laughing. At least she was not alone.

She felt something nudge her foot. It was the rabbit. It hopped through the doorway that divided the kitchen from the living room. Miranda followed it. The rabbit saw Miranda and hopped through her legs and back into the living room. Miranda stopped in the doorway between the living room and the kitchen. She walked back and forth. She looked at the two rooms. She considered the two different spaces.

Then Miranda had an idea.

@ @ @

Friday came quickly. That meant it was time for desk cleanup. Ms. Basil looked in everybody's desks. She was afraid to look in Miranda's. But Miranda just sat there, smiling.

"I hope there's nobody in your desk," Ms. Basil said.

Miranda pushed her chair back so Ms. Basil could inspect it. "Take a look."

Ms. Basil bent down to look inside. She stood there and stared into Miranda's desk. Her eyes went wide. "I don't believe it!"

Some students came rushing over. "Is Jaiden in the desk again?"

"I'm right here," Jaiden said. He stood beside Ms. Basil. "Wow!"

Now everyone in the class came running over.

Miranda's desk was totally tidy!

She had put a divider in the middle of her desk. Miranda's books were on one side. Her papers and pencils were on the other. This way, she knew where everything went.

"What a great idea," Ms. Basil said. "I should try that for my own desk."

"Really?" Jaiden said. "What's your desk like?"

Everybody looked at Ms. Basil's desk. It was in the back corner of the room. Ms. Basil always heaped student work onto it. It was piled high with papers, books and things for the classroom. It looked like a mountain.

"Oh," Ms. Basil said. Her face went red. "I guess it's *my* turn to stay in for recess today."

"Don't worry, Ms. Basil." Miranda smiled. "I'll give you a hand."

Jeff Szpirglas and Danielle Saint-Onge
live together in Toronto and teach in classrooms
with students of diverse cultural backgrounds. Jeff
has written several books, including the award-
nominated *You Just Can't Help It!* and a terrifying
new novel called *Evil Eye*. Danielle has a master's
degree in social anthropology and is a crusader for
equity in the classroom. Besides teaching, they spend
their time writing stories like *Something's Fishy* and
taking care of their twin babies.